Richard Scarry's
BEST LITTLE
WORD BOOK
EVER!

A GOLDEN BOOK • NEW YORK
Golden Books Publishing Company, Inc., New York, New York 10106

© 1992 Richard Scarry. All rights reserved. Printed in the U.S.A. No part of this book may be reproduced or copied in any form without written permission from the publisher. GOLDEN BOOKS®, A GOLDEN BOOK®, A LITTLE GOLDEN STORYBOOK™, G DESIGN™, and the distinctive gold spine are trademarks of Golden Books Publishing Company, Inc. Library of Congress Catalog Card Number: 97-70968   ISBN: 0-307-16055-6
First Little Golden Storybook Edition 1997   A MCMXCVIII

Huckle Cat says hello.
He wants you to meet
his sister Sally and his
good friend Lowly Worm.

jacket

sweater

Hi! I'm
Goldbug.

pants

mittens

Huckle

socks

sneakers

boots

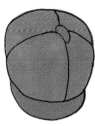

cap

blouse

raincoat

hat

dress

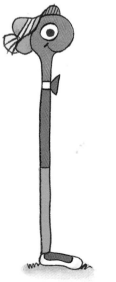

Here are the
clothes they wear.
Lowly wears only
one sneaker.

Lowly Worm

Sally

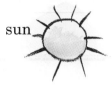
sun

The Cat family lives in a nice house. They are always busy doing things around the house.

Lowly is in bed because he is still tired. Sleep tight, Lowly.

Daddy

carpenter

bathroom

doorway

kitchen

pot

clock

Mommy

frying pan

measuring spoons

chair

eggbeater

strainer

drawers

clock

keys

dish rack

sink

double boiler

teapot

coffeepot

cup

saucer

fork

plate

egg

knife

spoon

In the kitchen, Daddy washes the dishes. Mommy fixes good things to eat. Mmm. Fresh strawberries.

lamp

strawberries

bowl

bread

glass of milk

sugar bowl

table

pitcher

butter

red fire engine

yellow school bus

The Cat family gets into the car and drives to town to go shopping.

What a busy street!

orange car

pink bug car

blue police car

brown truck

green pickle car

violet bug car

black-and-white taxi

police station

Daddy is driving the family to the supermarket. You're a good driver, Daddy.

street cleaner

stoplight

broom

curb

POST OFFICE

baby

stroller

sign SUPERMARKET

scale

grocer

butcher

sidewalk

At the supermarket,
Mommy and Sally
shop for food. Lowly
helps them.

pineapple

peaches

lemons

apples

oranges

cherries

plums

pears

melons

strawberries

blueberries

checkout person

cash register

pie

milk

can

bread

BIG LOAF

bag

grapes

peas

squash

bananas

grapefruit

corn

lettuce

beans

raspberries

tomatoes

beets

carrots

sack of potatoes

watermelon

Did Mommy forget anything?

cookies

sugar

cereal

eggs

smoke

fence

gate

farmhouse

water pump

ax

woodpile

Hello, Farmer Pig!
Farmer Pig grows all kinds
of fruits and vegetables
on his farm.

plow

tractor

scarecrow

hoe

ladder

shovel

barn

rake

rooster

chick

hen

vegetable garden

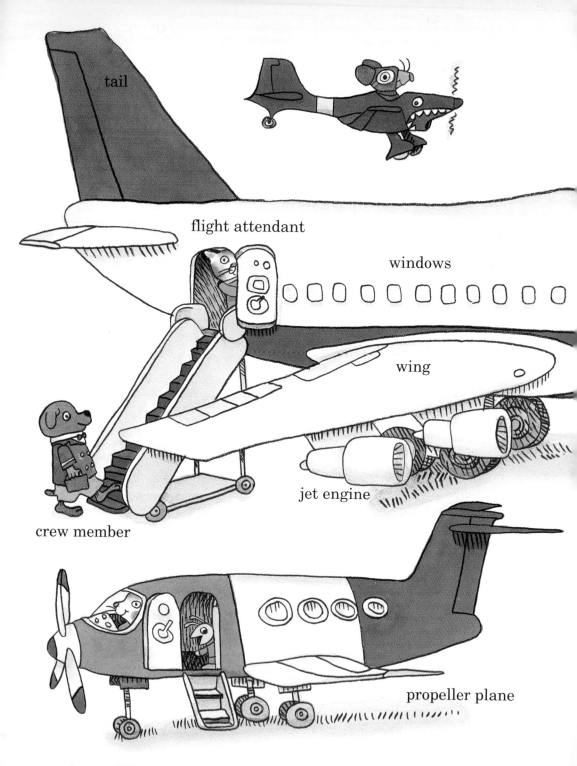

tail

flight attendant

windows

wing

crew member

jet engine

propeller plane

helicopter

cockpit

nose

jet airplane

wheel

two pilots

control tower

The airport is a busy place.
There are all kinds of airplanes.
Some are taking off, and some
are landing on the ground.
Would you like to fly in an
airplane?

flag

captain

smokestack

lifeboat

anchor

cargo ship

buoy

sail

fishing boat

sailboat

submarine

lighthouse

crane

cargo

dock

tugboat

raft

The harbor is filled with boats.
They have to be careful not to bump
into each other.

Here are the letters of the alphabet.

A a

apple car

bear

B b

E e

engine

fox

F f

I i

ice cream

J j

jeep

cat

Dd

Dingo Dog

Cc

goat

Gg

Hh

Hilda Hippo

Kk

kangaroo

Ll

Lowly

M m
motorcycle

N n
nurse

Q q
queen

R r
rooster

U u
umbrella

V v
violin

W w
wolf

O o

owl

P p

plump
penguin

S s

smiling sailor

T t

tiger

X x

xylophone

yak

Y y

zebra

Z z

Can you name all the parts of your body?

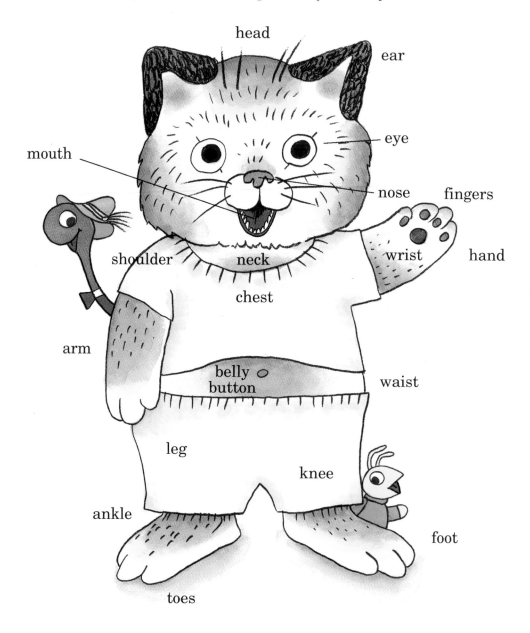

head

ear

mouth

eye

nose

fingers

shoulder

neck

wrist

hand

chest

arm

belly
button

waist

leg

knee

ankle

foot

toes

Now Huckle, Lowly Worm,
and Goldbug say good-bye to you.